W9-AVR-630

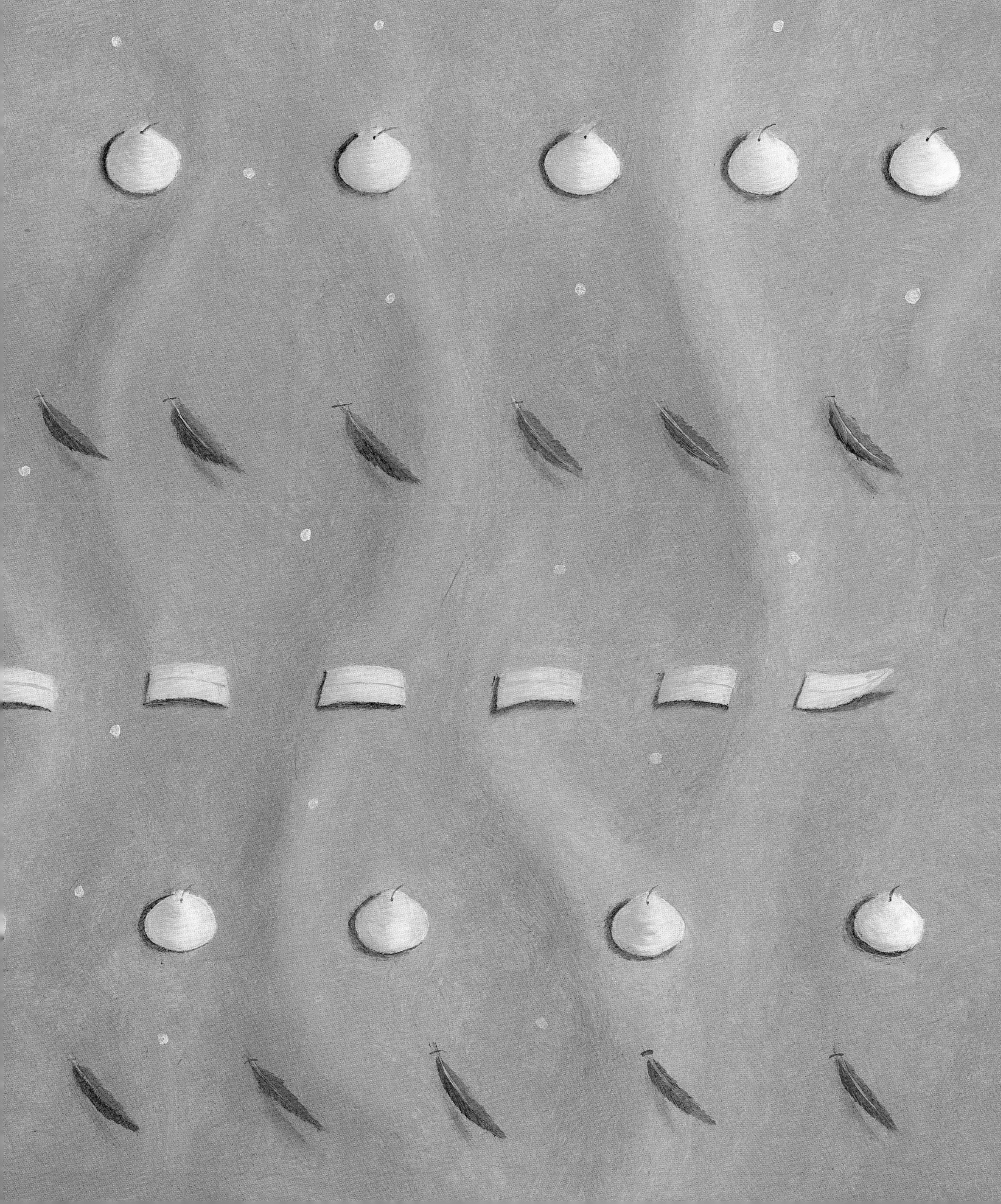

For Marian, who knits – M.D.
For Deborah – A.J.

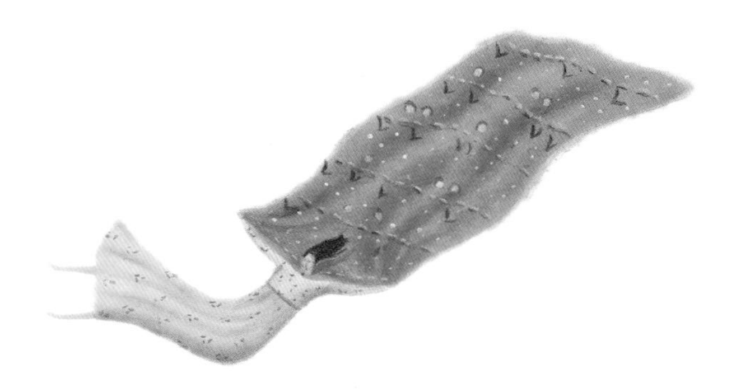

First published in Great Britain in 2004 by
Frances Lincoln Limited, 4 Torriano Mews
Torriano Avenue, London NW5 2RZ
www.franceslincoln.com

British Library Cataloguing in Publication Data
available on request

ISBN 0-7112-1962-1

Set in Goudy

Printed in Singapore

1 3 5 7 9 8 6 4 2

Visit the Malachy Doyle website at www.malachydoyle.co.uk

Una and the Sea-Cloak

Malachy Doyle
Illustrated by Alison Jay

FRANCES LINCOLN

One morning, after a great storm, Martin was down by the shore gathering driftwood, when a flash of green caught his eye. Hiding behind a rock, he was amazed to see a girl stagger out of the waves. Her long dark hair hung over a beautiful cloak, which clung like strips of green and silver seaweed to her thin body.

“How can I go home now my sea-cloak is in tatters?” the girl cried to the wind. Then she spread the shimmering cloth on the sand and lay down, exhausted.

Martin waited until she was asleep, and crept out from his hiding-place. He stood over her, fascinated by her beauty and by the delicacy of her cloak. But when he reached out to touch it, the girl sat up, fear flashing in her deep green eyes.

"It's all right," said Martin. "I won't hurt you."

"But look at my poor sea-cloak!" cried the girl, her tears falling to the sand. "The storm has ripped it to pieces."

"It's very beautiful," said Martin.

"It used to be," said the girl sadly. "When I wore it I could fly through the air, walk on land and swim to my home at the bottom of the ocean. Now that it's ruined, I can do nothing."

"Come with me to my mother," said Martin. "If anyone can fix your cloak, she can." So Una, for that was the girl's name, followed him to his cottage, where his mother fed her and put her to bed.

For two days and nights Una slept, while Martin's mother tried to mend the cloak.

"I cannot understand this cloth," she said, waking Una to give her food. "It neither dries nor mends."

"My grandmother made it from sea, air and land," Una murmured, falling back into a deep sleep.

That evening, Martin and his mother looked closely at the sea-cloak.

"There are strange grasses woven into it," said the woman. "Maybe if we can find more like them, and sew them in, it would give Una strength to walk."

"And here are some tiny green feathers," said Martin. "Would they help her to fly?"

"And little sparkling shells," said his mother, "so she can swim under the ocean."

"I will not rest," vowed the boy, "until I find them!"

Martin searched for a week and a day, until he came to a great bog. There in the middle were bulrushes, tall and proud, and among them the finest silver grasses.

"They're just like the ones in Una's cloak!" he cried, running towards them. But the mud gripped his legs and sucked him down, deeper and deeper.

Just in time, he grabbed hold of a branch of an old oak tree which leaned out over the bog, and pulled himself free. Then he climbed along the branch until he was low enough to pull up a clump of the silver grasses.

Martin took them to his mother, who sewed them into the cloak. Next morning, he draped it around Una's shoulders, and at once she opened her eyes.

"Where am I?" she asked.

"You're here with me and my mother," said Martin. "You've been very ill."

"Well, thank you for looking after me," said the girl, "but I must go home now, for my parents will be very worried."

She jumped up from her bed and ran outside.

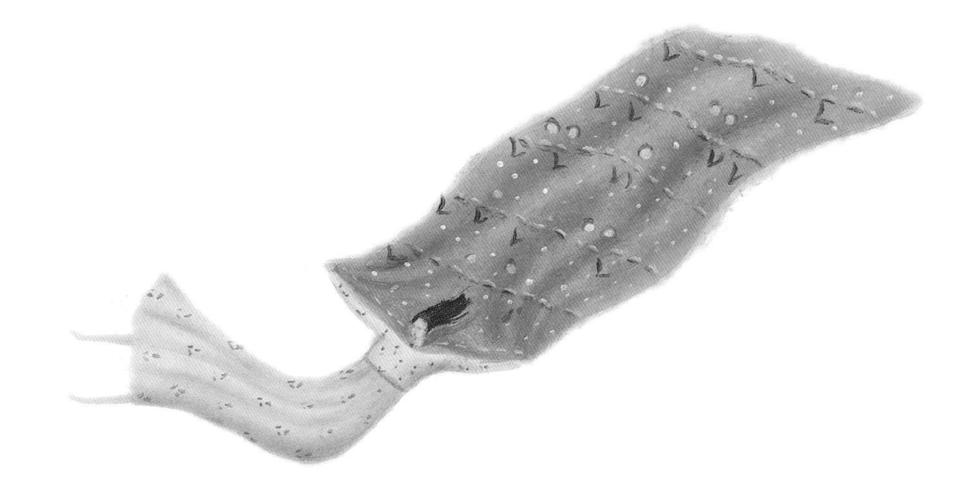

Climbing a high rock, she opened her arms wide, until the wind filled her cloak. Then she launched herself into the air, only to fall to the ground in a crumpled heap.

"I don't think your sea-cloak is quite ready, Una," said Martin, helping her up. "Maybe together we should try to find some of the tiny green feathers, and then you'll be able to fly."

So they searched and they searched for a week and a day. They found brown feathers, black feathers, red, white and blue feathers, but never a green one anywhere.

At last they came to a silent lake, high in the Mountains of Mourne.

Sitting by the water's edge, they heard the sound of geese flying overhead and watched as the whole flock swooped down beside them. Every goose was as green as the sea-cloak, and each one in turn presented Una and Martin with a delicate little breast feather.

"Oh, thank you," said Una, when they had returned to the cottage and Martin's mother had sewn the feathers into the cloth. "Now I can go back to my family."

She threw the cloak around her shoulders, climbed to the top of the high rock, stretched out her arms and flew.

"Has she gone for ever?" Martin asked his mother.

"I don't think so," the woman answered, "for we've still to find the shells."

And sure enough, there was Una, flying back out of the clouds.

"I've been to the ocean," she cried, sadly, "but I still can't swim underwater. Please help me."

So the next day Una and Martin climbed to the top of the great rock. They threw the sea-cloak around their shoulders, for with all the sewing it was now big enough for two, and off they flew.

They searched for a month and a week and a day, all around the coast of Ireland, until on a windswept shore they discovered thousands upon thousands of delicate little silver-green shells.

Scooping up as many of the shells as they could, they flew straight back to Martin's cottage, where his mother sewed them into the cloth.

"Will you be able to swim under the sea now, Una?" asked Martin the next morning.

"I do hope so," said the girl, throwing the sparkling cloak around her shoulders, "for I miss my parents sorely."

She stretched out her arms, soared through the air and dived straight down into the water.

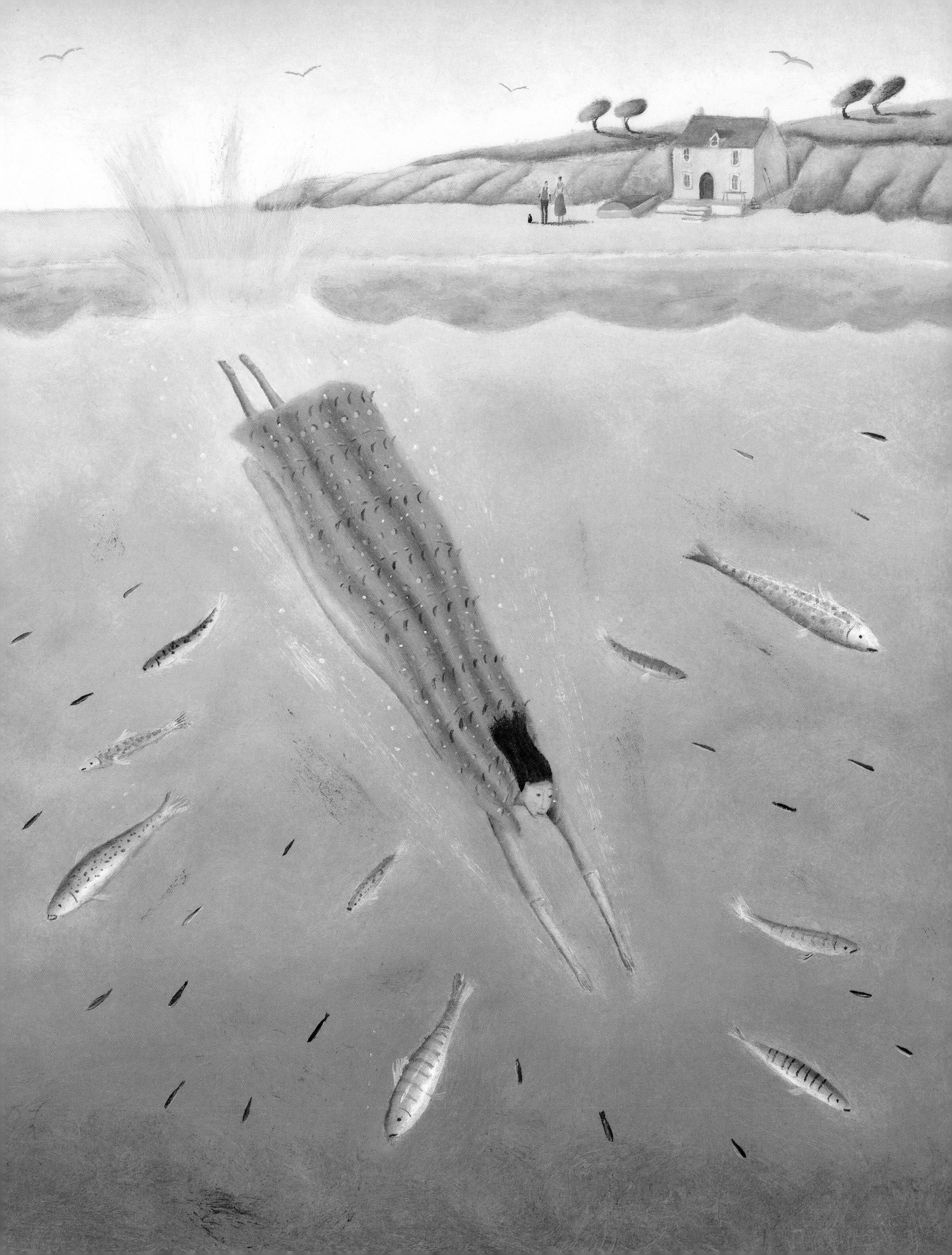

All day Martin sat on the rock, watching, but Una did not return.

In the evening, as the sun went down over the ocean, his mother came and stood by him.

"Look!" cried Martin, pointing out to sea. And there was Una, flashing out of the crimson sky.

“Come with me,” she called. “My parents want to thank you both. They’ve invited you to a great feast.” Spreading the cloak around Martin and his mother, she whisked them up and out and over the waves.

Down and down and down they went, until they came to a beautiful underwater palace.

"Welcome to our home," said Una's father, "and a hundred thousand thanks for saving our beloved daughter."

Martin and his mother gasped at the wonder of it all – the coral floors, the throne of gold and the table lit with a thousand pearls.

And when it was time to leave Una said, "I have a present for you, Martin. I hope you like it." And she gave him a sea-cloak, a sparkling new sea-cloak, so that he could fly in the air, swim under the sea and visit Una whenever he wished.

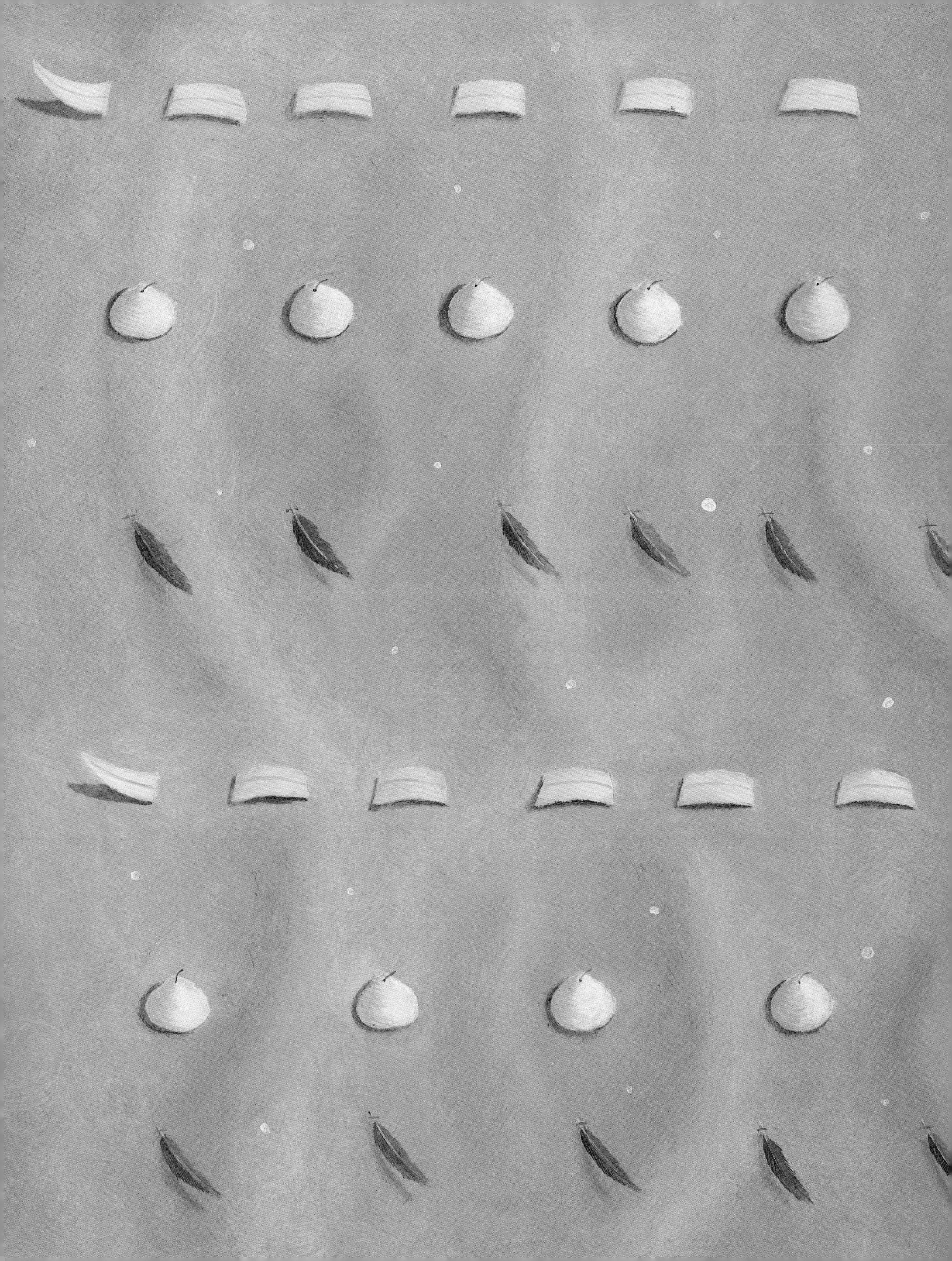